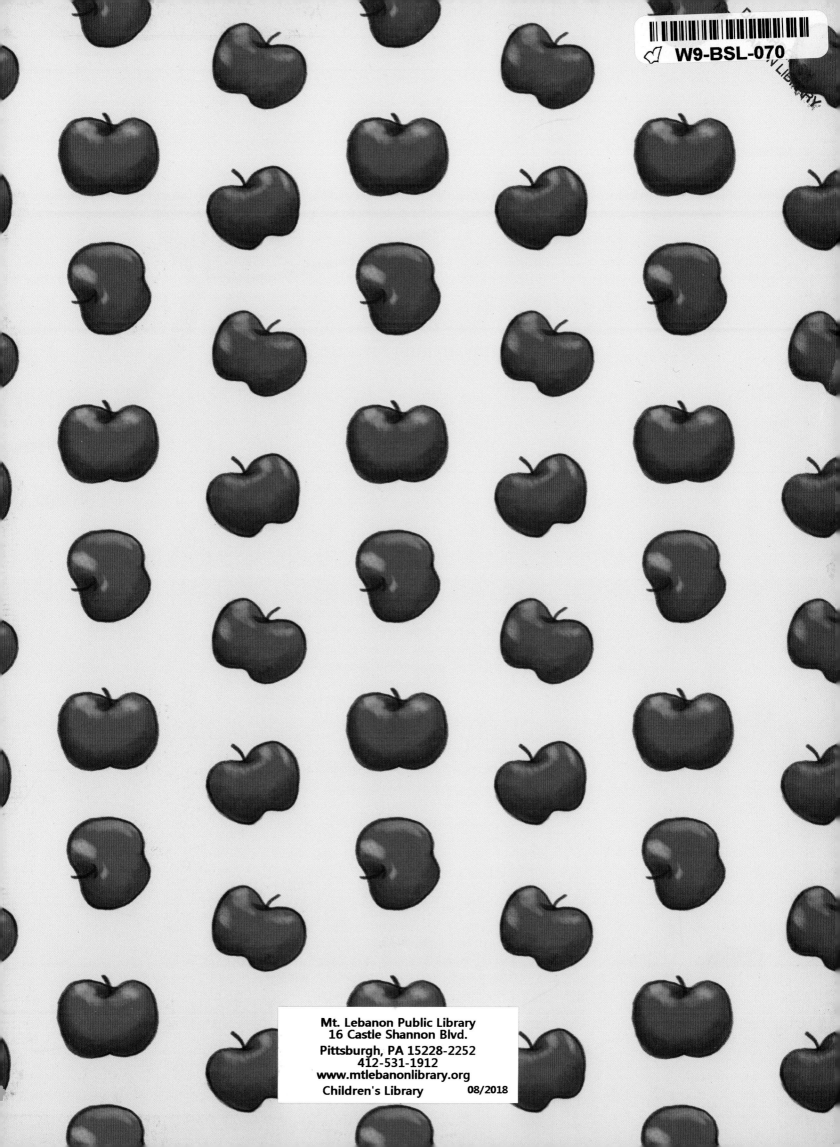

For Hoolie,
my lifelong favorite
—C. T.

For Christian,
the author pony
—J. S.

SIMON & SCHUSTER BOOKS FOR YOUNG READERS
An imprint of Simon & Schuster Children's Publishing Division
1230 Avenue of the Americas, New York, New York 10020
Text copyright © 2018 by Christian Trimmer
Illustrations copyright © 2018 by Jessie Sima
SIMON & SCHUSTER BOOKS FOR YOUNG READERS
is a trademark of Simon & Schuster, Inc.
For information about special discounts for bulk purchases, please contact Simon & Schuster Special Sales at
1-866-506-1949 or business@simonandschuster.com.
The Simon & Schuster Speakers Bureau can bring authors to your live event.
For more information or to book an event, contact the Simon & Schuster Speakers Bureau
at 1-866-248-3049 or visit our website at www.simonspeakers.com.
Book design by Lizzy Bromley
The text for this book was set in Fnord Seventeen.
The illustrations for this book were rendered in Adobe Photoshop.
Manufactured in China · 0418 SCP · First Edition
2 4 6 8 10 9 7 5 3 1
Library of Congress Cataloging-in-Publication Data
Names: Trimmer, Christian, author. | Sima, Jessie, illustrator.
Title: Snow Pony and the seven miniature ponies / Christian Trimmer ; illustrated by Jessie Sima.
Description: First Edition. | New York : Simon & Schuster Books for Young Readers, [2017] | Summary: In this
twist on the story of Snow White, pretty and sweet Snow Pony—beloved by children for her talent in braiding hair
and dancing—follows a trail of delicious apples into the woods, where she meets seven miniature ponies.
Identifiers: LCCN 2017044202 | ISBN 9781481462686 (hc) | 9781481462693 (eBook)
Subjects: | CYAC: Ponies—Fiction. | Friendship—Fiction.
Classification: LCC PZ7.1.T75 Sn 2017 | DDC [E]—dc23
LC record available at https://lccn.loc.gov/2017044202

Snow Pony

and the

Seven Miniature Ponies

Written by Christian Trimmer

Illustrated by Jessie Sima

Simon & Schuster Books for Young Readers

New York · London · Toronto · Sydney · New Delhi

Once upon a time

there was a pony who had a coat as white as snow and a mane as black as ebony. (As you can see, the combination was quite spectacular.) Her name was Snow Pony.

Children came from far and wide to see Snow Pony. Not only was she pretty and sweet, but she was also exceptionally good at braiding hair and line dancing. All the children loved Snow Pony, and she loved them all in return.

That's not entirely true. She didn't particularly like this one.

As long as we're being honest, Snow Pony *did*
have a favorite. Charmaine lived in the house on
the farm, and besides being gentle and kind, she
had a lovely singing voice.

Along with Charmaine's dog, Hunter (don't be
fooled by his name—the only thing Hunter hunted
was belly rubs), Snow Pony and Charmaine would
put on shows for the visiting children.

To be fair, there *was* one animal who did not like Snow Pony. Her name was Queenie, and she was jealous of all the attention Snow Pony received. Queenie had special talents of her own (or so she claimed) and was eager to show them off.

But she knew she would never have the chance . . . unless she got rid of Snow Pony.

The opportunity presented itself one day when the gate was mistakenly left unlocked.

One by one, Snow Pony ate the apples Queenie had placed in a trail that led deep into the forest.

Before long, Snow Pony was completely and utterly lost. She was also grumpy, agitated, irritable, and ill-tempered (all consequences of eating too many apples). Slowly, Snow Pony began to realize that she had been tricked.

The sun was beginning to set, and the forest became darker and darker. Snow Pony was scared. *How will I ever find my way home?* she wondered. Thankfully, just then, she stumbled into a clearing . . .

. . . and found herself at the entrance of a stable of modest stature.

There she discovered seven bales of hay, seven troughs, seven carrots, and seven stalls. Usually, Snow Pony would have noticed such an important detail, maybe even connected it to a story about a princess and some dwarves Charmaine had once told her. But at that moment Snow Pony discovered a cabinet full of sugar cubes. *I'll have just one*, she thought.

Feeling safe and warm, Snow Pony settled down in the seventh stall and was almost immediately asleep.

Not long after, the owners of the stable returned home.
They were seven miniature ponies, who, aside from being
adorable, were also very observant.

"Someone has been
nibbling at my hay!"

"Someone has been
drinking from my trough!"

"Someone has taken a
bite from my carrot!"

"Someone has eaten
one, two, three . . .
seventy-seven sugar cubes!"

"Someone has been
sleeping in my stall . . .

. . . and she still is! And right on top of my favorite blankie."

The miniature ponies had never seen a pony so beautiful (or large). They agreed to let her sleep.

The next morning Snow Pony awakened to the sight of seven pairs of eyes watching her. "Oh my!" she said.

"Do not be alarmed," said one of the miniature ponies. "You are safe here. What is your name?"

"Snow Pony," said Snow Pony. She told them how she had ended up lost in the forest.

"That Queenie sounds like a piece of work," said one of the miniature ponies. "You are welcome to stay as long as you want."

The miniature ponies explained how they each
contributed to the success of their stable.

"I gather water." "I take care
of the bees." "I'm a tax
attorney." "I collect
honey."

"I tend the herb garden."

"I grow the carrots."

"And *I* keep the sugar cabinet stocked. I've got my eye on you."

Snow Pony thought about her duties back on the farm and smiled. "I can help too!"

Day after day the
miniature ponies
left for their jobs . . .

And night after night they
returned for evenings packed

The miniature ponies had never been happier. Snow Pony, too, was happy to have so many new friends, but none of the miniature ponies could hit the high notes like Charmaine.

Back at Snow Pony's stable, the children had never been *less* happy. Queenie had taken Snow Pony's place, and the kids found her "talents" a bit wanting.

Charmaine shook her head. "This isn't good, boy. We need to find Snow Pony."

"I am in full agreement!" replied Hunter. "Let us depart at once! With my keen eyes and sense of smell, we are sure to find her in no time. And what a sight for sore eyes she will be! Oh yes, a joyful reunion we shall have."

Of course, what Charmaine heard was . . .

Bark! Bark!

Still, she recognized something in the dog's eyes. So the two raced off into the forest.

At that very same moment Snow Pony made a decision. "Dear miniature ponies," she said. "I must return home. You have been wonderful friends, but I miss the children, especially Charmaine."

The miniature ponies were devastated.

"Please don't go—you have brought so much joy into this house!" said one.

"My mane has never looked better!" cried another.

"I'm so close to learning the electric slide!" shouted a third.

Snow Pony looked into their sad, adorable eyes. "What if . . . you came with me? There's plenty of room on the farm! Charmaine and I could work you into our act!"

The miniature ponies considered her very tempting offer. "But what about our stable here?" asked the miniature pony who was also the tax attorney.

"Well," replied Snow Pony, "you could always use it as a weekend home. And maybe you could rent it for short periods of time to miniature ponies visiting the area who are looking for something more cozy than a hotel. I heard that's very popular these days."

The tax attorney's eyes lit up. "It's settled, then! We will join Snow Pony on her return home!"

With that, Snow Pony and the seven miniature ponies ventured into the thick forest.

Branches grabbed at Snow Pony's mane, and briars snagged at her ankles. The miniature ponies, who had never traveled this far, were faring even worse. The group stopped to rest.

"I will run ahead to see what I can learn," offered the miniature pony who took care of the bees.

Just a few minutes later he came speeding back. "We must hide! I've just seen a hairless monster who walks on two legs and a slobbery beast with sharp fangs!"

Snow Pony and the miniature ponies scrambled to get out of sight.

Snow Pony's heart was pounding. The rustle of leaves and the snap of twigs announced the arrival of the monster and beast. The beast began to bark and the monster was singing. The sounds were terrifying . . . and familiar. *Wait a second,* Snow Pony thought.

She peeked out from her hiding spot. Could it be . . . ?

It was! Her beloved Charmaine and Hunter!

She raced to her friends, and the three of them embraced.

"Snow Pony," said Charmaine, "I thought I'd never see you again. Why did you leave us?"

"My dear Charmaine! I would never willingly leave you. I was tricked by that mean ol' Queenie. She lured me out of the stable and deep into the woods. I became oh-so lost and oh-so scared! But I thought of you every day, and I dreamed of this very moment."

Of course, all Charmaine heard was . . .

Neigh!

"You can come out!" Snow Pony called to the miniature ponies. "This is Charmaine and Hunter, a child and a dog, not a monster and a beast. You guys really need to get out more."

One by one, the seven miniature ponies revealed themselves.

"My goodness!" exclaimed Charmaine. "You've brought some friends!"

Charmaine, Snow Pony, and Hunter happily returned home with the miniature ponies in tow. From that day forward, life on the farm was better—and busier—than ever. Children came from even farther and wider to see the pony with a coat as white as snow and a mane as black as ebony perform alongside her best friend and seven miniature ponies.

Snow Pony loved all the children, just as they loved her. Well, you know, except this one.

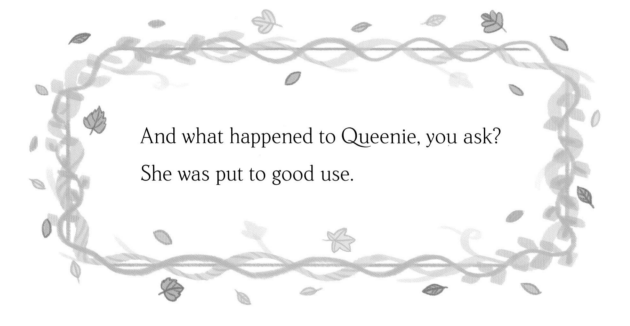

And what happened to Queenie, you ask?

She was put to good use.